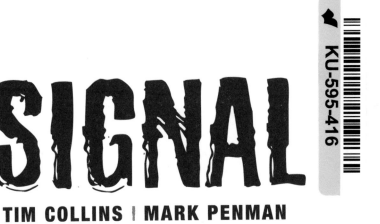

SIGNAL

TIM COLLINS | MARK PENMAN

"… it feels like there's something wrong with this place.
It's hard to explain."

Badger
LEARNING

Signal ISBN 978-1-78837-528-3

Publisher / Senior Editor: Danny Pearson
Editor: Claire Wood
Copyeditor: Cheryl Lanyon
Designer: Bigtop Design Ltd
Illustration: Mark Penman

2 4 6 8 10 9 7 5 3 1

CHAPTER 1
DISTRESS SIGNAL

"The lady two floors below us is upset," said Mei. "She's been sad all day."

"Try not to worry about it," said Nikko. "Get some sleep."

Nikko listened out for sobbing, but he could hear nothing except the low hum of the spaceship. His sister could sense the feelings of anyone near. It was a power that had got them both into a lot of trouble back on Earth, and he wanted her to give it a rest.

"A man on this floor is very angry," said Mei.

"There are a lot of people on this ship," said Nikko. "Try not to think about how they're all feeling."

They'd been on the passenger ship for almost a week now. It would still be three months until they reached their new home on the Roku colony. Mei was going to make herself ill if she didn't stop taking on the pain of others.

"But the angry man is coming right towards us," said Mei. "He's here now."

The door to their cabin swung open. Nikko was sure he'd locked it from the inside. Whoever this was had access to the whole ship.

A man wearing a black uniform and carrying a large machine gun walked in. He threw up his visor and fixed his fierce eyes on Mei, ignoring Nikko.

"I need your help," he said. "Come with me."

Nikko stood up, blocking the man's line of sight.

"We're passengers on this ship," he said. "We've paid for our tickets and you don't have the right to make us do anything."

The man stared at Nikko. He moved his right hand, and for a moment Nikko thought he was going to shoot him. But instead he pulled an ID card out of his pocket.

It read:
Hiro Tanaka
Security Officer
Ichi Corporation

"I have every right to ask for your sister's help," he said. "And I was talking to her and not you, so please step aside."

Nikko sighed. However hard he tried to keep his sister's talent secret, there was always someone who knew about it.

Mei climbed down from her bunk and swept her long black hair back behind her ears.

"I'd better go with him," she said. "He's very angry. And also quite scared."

Hiro looked at her in confusion and Nikko grinned.

"She doesn't always tell you what you want to hear, does she?" Nikko asked. "But she's always right. So this really is an emergency, then?"

"No," said Hiro, still looking at Mei as if she'd bitten him. "It's probably nothing."

Mei lifted her grey body suit from the peg next to her bunk and stepped into it. She dragged the zip up and fixed a strap across the collar.

"This morning we received a distress signal from a cargo ship returning from Hachi, the new colony," said Hiro. "My guess is that it was sent by mistake, but we've got to check it out. Corporation rules."

Mei stepped towards Hiro, but Nikko stuck his arm out to stop her.

"It wasn't safe for my sister on Earth," said Nikko. "Too many people wanted to use her skills for their own gain. That's why we've left Earth. Now the same thing is happening."

Hiro stepped forwards until his visor was level with the top of Nikko's head. Nikko could smell the coffee on his breath.

"Were you even listening?" he asked. "I'm answering a distress signal. To see if I can help someone. Not for my own gain. If someone really is trapped on that ship, it will be much easier for me to find them if your sister is there."

Nikko backed away. He didn't like Hiro's aggressive tone, but he had to agree. He was asking Mei to help someone who might be suffering. It would be selfish of them to refuse.

"OK," said Nikko. "But I'm coming too."

He grabbed his crumpled body suit from the floor. He sat on the edge of his bunk, dragged the trouser legs over his feet, then stood up and pulled the sleeves on. He was dreading going to the cargo ship, but he couldn't let Mei go without him. If there was something dangerous, he wanted to be there to help her.

He noticed that Mei was staring at him. He always felt uncomfortable when she did that.

"You're frightened too now," she said. "Should I be frightened?"

"No," he said.

But there was no point lying to his sister. He'd learned that a long time ago.

CHAPTER 2
ABANDONED

Nikko felt the shuttle jolt into place as it docked with the cargo ship. It had taken Hiro just thirty minutes to get them there.

Hiro had been piloting the small craft. Mei and Nikko were strapped into seats against the right side.

Nikko unbuckled himself and watched as Hiro walked over to the thick metal door on the left. He pulled down a handle and slid it open. Nikko could make out the black floor and high walls of the docking bay beyond.

"Hello?" shouted Hiro.

There was no response.

They stepped out into the vast, empty space. There were other docking ports on either side of them, but both were empty. According to a sign on the wall, they were on level two. There were three levels above them and two below them. The ship was huge, bigger even than the one they'd come from.

They followed Hiro through a large doorway into a corridor lined with big rooms. He clanged on every door with the butt of his gun and shouted, "Hello?"

There was no sound except for the buzzing of the lights and the chugging of the air generators.

Hiro turned around to Mei.

"Do you feel anything?" he asked. "Can you sense anyone?"

"No," said Mei. "I don't think so."

Hiro strode over to a glass panel set into the wall next to one of the doors. He smashed it with the end of his gun and grabbed a red lever inside.

"Cover your ears," he said.

Nikko clasped his hands to the sides of his head.

Hiro yanked the switch and it let out a high, screeching alarm. After a few seconds, he pulled it up again.

"There," he said. "If there's anyone on the ship, they'll know where we are."

Nikko peered down the long corridor, waiting for dark figures to appear around the corner. No one came.

"My guess is that the ship broke down and was abandoned," said Hiro. "The distress signal set itself off by mistake as the computers died."

"So we can go back now?" asked Nikko.

Hiro shook his head.

"We have to cover the whole place," he said. "Corporation rules. We have to make sure someone isn't in need of our help."

He turned to Mei.

"Let me know if you get anything," he said. "Anything at all."

Mei nodded.

They set off down the murky corridor. Nikko could feel himself tensing up as he imagined shapes emerging from the gloom. Maybe a lone survivor with wide eyes and bitten fingers, driven to madness by being trapped here alone.

But there was nothing to worry about. Mei would know if someone was close.

Despite this, a thought popped into Nikko's mind and he felt his muscles tighten even more.

Mei would know if any people were close, but what if something that wasn't human was lurking on the ship? What if some huge creature was waiting for them in the shadows? Would it rip their necks open right away or would it torture them first to amuse itself?

Nikko told his brain to stop. There were no bug-eyed monsters lurking in space. It had been fifty years since the first colony was set up, and no alien life forms had been discovered.

Or, at least, none they'd been told about.

There was a loud pop overhead and Nikko couldn't stop himself jumping. A strip light flickered into life before shutting off again.

"This whole place is falling apart," said Hiro. "No wonder the distress signal set itself off."

This didn't help. Instead of imagining crouching creatures, Nikko now imagined the roof collapsing, the air failing, or the thick metal doors locking themselves shut. The sooner they searched this place and got back to the shuttle, the better.

Hiro stared at Mei.

"Still not getting anything?" he asked.

"I don't think so," she said. "But it feels like there's something wrong with this place. It's hard to explain."

"I'm sure plenty of things went wrong," he said. "That's why they abandoned the ship."

Some of the doors they were passing had long windows. Nikko couldn't make out much inside except for some ripped cardboard boxes and torn plastic packaging. He guessed these rooms had stored the building panels that were shipped to the colony.

Thinking about the construction workers stepping out onto the distant moon to set up the first houses made him shiver. What if they'd disturbed something? Maybe that was the real reason their journey home was interrupted?

Nikko told himself to stop. He could make up fairy stories later when they were safely back on the passenger ship. For now, he just had to keep himself together.

The corridor ended in a large, empty space with a doorway to the left. Nikko could make out a stairwell through a square window.

Hiro glanced back at Mei.

"How about we go down and then up the stairs and see if you feel something?" asked Hiro. "That should speed things up."

"OK," said Mei, sweeping her hair back from her face. Nikko noticed that her hands were trembling.

Hiro pushed open the door with his foot and stuck his gun through into the stairwell. The barrel had a light on the end, and he swept it back and forth before going in. Nikko wondered if he'd been in the army before working as a security officer.

Hiro clanked down the metal stairs and Nikko and Mei followed. They passed a sign marking level one.

Hiro looked at Mei, but she shook her head.

They kept on going. The stairs ended on level zero. Beyond the doors to their left was a long corridor lined with escape pods. The green lights above their metal doors indicated they were all docked and ready to use.

"So they didn't abandon the ship," said Mei. "The pods are still here."

Nikko felt sweat trickling down his forehead and his back. His sister was right. This didn't fit with Hiro's idea at all.

"A ship like this would have plenty of escape pods," said Hiro. "So what if they didn't use these ones?"

"You feel unsure," said Mei. "You don't really know if that's true."

Hiro span around to face Mei and his arm twitched as if he were about to aim his gun at her. She flinched and Nikko leapt in between them.

"I didn't bring you here to tell me how I feel," Hiro said. "You're here to help me find out if there's someone on this ship."

He pointed back to the door. "So let's keep going," he said.

Hiro climbed the stairs with both hands on his gun. Nikko rushed to catch up with him.

"Mei is right about the escape pods," said Nikko. "Your story about the crew abandoning this ship doesn't work. Why don't we go back, report it to the Corporation, and let them send out an army ship?"

"They don't need the army," said Hiro. "They sent me. And I'm not returning until we know exactly what happened."

They stomped up the stairs, past level three. Level four was marked as Lower Living Quarters. Nikko smelt rotting meat as they passed it, perhaps the remains of discarded meals.

Level five was marked with a sign that read Upper Living Quarters. As they approached it, Mei let out a cry.

"Getting something?" asked Hiro. "Good."

"No," said Mei. She was frozen halfway up the stairs. "It's not good. Someone is close. They feel… I don't know… they're struggling. That's all I can tell."

"I'm not surprised they're struggling if they've been stuck on here for weeks," said Hiro. "Let's go and find them."

Mei cowered back, pushing herself to the wall.

"No!" said Mei. "We need to go back. We're in danger."

CHAPTER 3
SURVIVOR

Hiro pushed open the door to level five. Mei was still halfway down the stairs. Nikko was next to her with his arm around her shoulders.

"Come on," said Hiro. "Let's see who's here and then we can go."

He swung his gun around until it was almost pointing towards them. He didn't need to threaten them. Nikko knew they had no choice but to follow.

Hiro stuck his head through the door.

"Hello?" he shouted. "I'm a security officer from the Ichi Corporation. I'm responding to a distress signal."

There was no reply.

They stepped slowly along the corridor. Hiro went in front, grasping his gun. Nikko followed, still with an arm around his sister's shoulder.

Level five had a dull, grey carpet and green walls. It was lit by bright overhead lights and there were safety notices pinned up. There was a coffee vending machine with a fire extinguisher to the left and a water fountain to the right.

Nikko could see small bedrooms through the windows in the doors. There were metal beds with thin mattresses, tables covered in papers and coffee cups. The walls had children's drawings and family photographs taped on them.

Only one of the bedrooms had a light on. It was halfway down on the left.

"That's where the struggle is coming from," said Mei. "We shouldn't approach. It's too dangerous."

Nikko could feel his sister's shoulders trembling. He was dragging rather than guiding her now. He thought about making a run for it. He didn't believe Hiro would actually shoot them. They could go back and let Hiro face this alone.

But what use would that be? Neither of them could fly a shuttle. They'd end up lost in space and starving to death.

"Let me worry about the danger," said Hiro, tapping the side of his gun.

They approached the door with the light shining through.

"Hello?" shouted Hiro. "We got your distress signal."

The door was pulled slowly open.

Nikko noticed that Hiro's finger was on the trigger of his gun. He was ready to attack.

Nikko could feel his heart speeding. His sister's breathing was getting faster and faster. His body tensed, ready to run if some vicious creature emerged.

A man stepped out. He was wearing a thin, white T-shirt and blue shorts. His black hair was overgrown and he had a messy beard.

"Thank you for coming," he said, pushing his face into a wide grin. "I'm so glad you got my signal."

Hiro turned around and shrugged at Mei.

"He doesn't look very dangerous," he said.

"He is," whispered Mei. "He's as dangerous as a whole army."

The man walked forwards, holding his hands up.

"I'm unarmed," he said. "Just an ordinary ship's mechanic, asking for your help."

Hiro tilted his gun up at the man's face.

"If my friend says you're dangerous, we'll assume you are," he said. "We don't know anything about you. Why are you alone? Where is everyone?"

The man looked down at Hiro's gun and his smile drooped. Nikko could see the man's skin sagging under his mouth and eyes, as if he'd suddenly grown 20 years older.

The man forced his smile back into place.

"The others were picked up by a rescue ship," he said. "They left me behind because I was still trying to fix our engines. I thought I could save them. It turns out I was wrong."

Nikko gazed at him, waiting for his face to fall again. It stayed frozen in a smile, but his cheeks and forehead twitched with the effort.

"So will you take me?" the man asked. "Those are the Corporation's rules aren't they?"

"OK," said Hiro. "Let's head for the docking bay. You go ahead and we'll follow. But I'm going to cuff your hands and feet before you get into our ship. OK?"

The man nodded and walked past them, still smiling. The stench of stale meat filled Nikko's nostrils.

The man limped along the corridor in front of them.

Hiro went next, keeping his gun aimed at the man's back. Nikko and Mei hung further behind.

"I don't want to get into that tiny shuttle with him," whispered Nikko. "I don't care if he has handcuffs on."

"His whole body is filled with the struggle," said Mei. "He feels like he'll explode."

Nikko watched the man as he staggered down the corridor. He didn't know exactly what his sister meant, but if the man was going to lose it, he should do it here and not in their shuttle. If he went crazy in the shuttle, Hiro would be too busy at the controls to deal with him.

Nikko wanted to tip him over the edge now.
But how could he do it?

He looked around the corridor. There was the vending machine. Perhaps he could drench him in hot coffee? No, that would take too long to pour, so it wouldn't be much of a surprise.

His eyes fixed on the fire extinguisher.
That could work.

"I'm going to try something," he whispered to Mei. "Stay back here."

Nikko unhooked the fire extinguisher. It was a small rectangle of black metal with a red button on one end and a wide nozzle on the other.
He held it up and charged forwards.

He barged past Hiro and fired it at the limping man.

Gas hissed out. The limping man turned around and let out a deep, rasping scream.

His eye sockets turned to lifeless white blanks. The skin below them fell loose, and blood trickled down his cheeks in jagged lines. His mouth dropped and his head rolled to the side.

Nikko could see a black creature inside the man's mouth. It had large, insect eyes and long, thin claws.

Hiro was staring at it in shock. His whole body was completely frozen. Nikko had to prod him.

"What are you waiting for?" he shouted. "That thing isn't human."

The man's arms and legs were shaking uncontrollably and his head was juddering back and forth.

"The man has gone now," said Mei. "I'm not getting any feelings from him."

Nikko shoved Hiro on the arm. This was enough to snap him out of his trance. He pulled the trigger and fired three bullets into the man's chest.

The man collapsed. The black creature crawled out of his mouth. It had a long, winding body lined with legs, like a huge centipede. Below its deep, black eyes were a row of white, almost human teeth.

Another creature burst out of the bullet wound in the man's chest. A smaller one burrowed out of his left calf, cutting its way free with its sharp claws.

The three creatures scuttled across the floor towards them.

"Run!" shouted Nikko.

He grabbed Mei's wrist and dragged her down the corridor.

CHAPTER 4
ESCAPE ROUTE

Hiro hurtled through the door and slammed his weight against it. They'd retreated to the far end of the corridor and into another stairwell.

"I think I shot all three of those things," said Hiro, gasping to get his breath back. "But I'm not sure."

He turned to Mei. "Can you sense anything back there?"

"No," said Mei. "I got nothing from the man when the creatures took over. I could sense his struggle until he lost control."

Hiro stepped back from the door and peered through its rectangular window into the bright, carpeted corridor.

"Nothing moving," he said. "But we'd better not risk it. More of those things could have crawled out of what's left of him."

He pointed down the stairwell. "This way," he said.

Nikko grabbed the handrail and stepped slowly down.

The light was dimmer than in the corridor. Single bulbs covered in wire mesh lined the sloping roof. There were dark shadows in every corner and Nikko couldn't stop himself imagining those creatures leaping out of them. A lurching feeling filled his stomach as he thought about their black eyes and white teeth.

"What were they?" asked Nikko.

"Some sort of parasite," said Hiro. "They were living inside that man and controlling him. I've never heard of anything like it. When this gets back to the Corporation, they'll want to destroy this whole ship. They won't take any chances."

"Good," said Nikko.

They followed the stairs around a bend. Nikko clung on to the inner handrail, still watching the shadows.

"Will we have to come back to this ship again?" asked Mei. "I don't want to come back here."

"No," said Hiro. "But I expect you'll both have to return to Earth to give evidence, I'm afraid."

Nikko felt his heart sink. Just when he thought they'd escaped Earth, they'd be sent straight back to that sweltering, overcrowded place. Even worse, if they had to visit the Corporation buildings, it would mean staying in Tokyo. Mei would be able to feel the pain of thousands of people all at once in such a big city. Every day would be agony for her.

He told himself that a big city was the least of his worries right now. First they had to get off the ship without running into any more of those things.

They reached another landing. There was a Lower Living Quarters sign, just like the one they'd seen earlier.

"We passed this corridor on the other side," said Hiro. "It should be easy to get back to where we were."

Nikko peered through the square window in the door. The corridor looked almost identical to the one above, with a grey carpet, green walls and bright overhead lights.

Hiro pushed the door open and they stepped in.

"This place feels bad," said Mei. "I don't think we should be here."

"This whole ship is bad," said Nikko. "Let's take the quickest route out."

They crept along the corridor. The same rotting smell came back to Nikko. It was even stronger than before.

The passage was lined with dark bedrooms, just as the other had been. But this time there were no lights on in any of them.

Nikko heard a low thudding noise in the room to his right and felt his skin prickle. He told himself not to worry. It was probably just a coffee cup, finally rolling off the table weeks after being abandoned.

They reached the mid-point of the corridor and Mei let out a whimper. She stopped, glancing over her shoulder.

"Come on," said Nikko. "We need to keep going."

"I'm feeling the struggle again," said Mei. "It's much stronger now."

Nikko's stomach squirmed as he thought about the slimy black creatures. He looked around. One of the doors behind them seemed to have opened slightly. He could have been imagining it, but he didn't want to stick around to find out. He grabbed Mei's hand and pulled her down the corridor.

Hiro was racing ahead. He was almost at the end of the corridor when two doors on either side of him sprung open. A man emerged from the one on the left, and a woman came out of the one on the right, blocking Hiro's way.

The man and woman were both wearing grey jumpsuits with the Ichi Corporation logo on the pockets. Their mouths were slack and drooping, but they forced them into wide grins.

"We're so glad you've come to rescue us," said the man.

"Please take us back to your ship," said the woman.

This time Hiro didn't try and speak to them. He fired first at the man, then at the woman. The blasts sent them into the walls, then their bodies crumpled forwards onto the carpet. The man fell face down, while the woman fell on top of him with her arm draped to the side.

Nikko watched as a pair of claws burrowed out of the woman's forearm. It was a smaller centipede creature, maybe a baby one. The thought made him feel sick. Four larger creatures burst out of the two bodies and scuttled forwards.

Hiro picked them off one by one, hitting his target every time. Their bodies exploded, spraying stinking green liquid on the walls and floor.

Nikko felt a hand on his back. Mei was shoving him. She was pointing at the ceiling with her other hand.

"Watch out!" she cried.

Nikko looked up and saw one of the creatures dangling over his head, its sharp claws snapping.

He leapt away before it could pounce.

There was a flurry of movement behind them. All the doors seemed to be opening at once. Four men and three women stepped out of the dark rooms. All were limping, and all were grinning.

"This way!" yelled Hiro. He beckoned them towards the end of the corridor where the bodies of the first man and woman were lying.

Nikko grabbed Mei's wrist and pulled her past Hiro, who immediately started firing. Nikko could hear raspy screams, just like the one the first man had made.

He didn't want to hang around near the bodies. There could be more of those black creatures still inside them, waiting to crawl out. The safest thing to do was to get back to the shuttle and wait for Hiro.

Nikko could hear Hiro's gun firing as they ran down the stairs. The noise cut out as they reached the second level.

"I hope he hasn't run out of bullets," he said.

"He's very frightened," said Mei.

They darted past the dark storerooms and back to the docking bay.

Nikko reached the shuttle first. He pulled up the metal handle, slid open the door and waited for Mei to bundle in. He kept his eyes fixed on the black floor to make sure none of the creatures had followed them.

When Mei was in, he slammed the door shut.

The controls of the craft were on his left. Two steering wheels, three rows of switches, a control screen and an overhead panel were placed around two observation windows.

"If Hiro doesn't come back, we're going to have to try and work all that out," said Nikko, waving his hand at the controls.

"You're worried about it," said Mei.

Nikko couldn't stop himself letting out a snigger, despite everything.

"No kidding," he said. "I'd never even been in a shuttle before today, and now I'm talking about flying one. How do you think I feel?"

He looked over at the screen. It was black now, but when Hiro had been using it, it had been a bright jumble of instructions and symbols. He wondered how he'd ever make any sense out of it.

If he could get autopilot going, maybe it would take the shuttle near enough to their ship for someone to come out and help. That's if he could work out how to undock the ship without crashing.

"Wait" said Mei, lifting her hand in the air. "Someone's coming."

Nikko listened out for footsteps, but could hear nothing but his own breathing.

"I can feel fear," said Mei. "It's getting closer."

"Let's hope it's Hiro," said Nikko, "and not another crew member."

Now he could hear footsteps. Distant metal clangs at first, the sound of someone on the stairwell. Then faint thuds in the corridor, then louder ones in the docking bay.

Someone smacked the outside of the door.

"Hello?" asked Nikko.

He could feel his heart thumping as he listened out for more raspy screaming.

"Let me in!" said a muffled voice. It was Hiro.

Nikko pulled down the handle and opened the door just enough for Hiro to squeeze through.

Hiro was dripping with sweat, and his uniform and visor were splashed with vile green liquid. He'd lost his gun and his trousers were ripped.

He leant forwards to get his breath back.

"I ran out of bullets," he said. "I squashed them with the end of my gun for a while, but there were too many. Let's go."

Hiro stumbled over to the front seat and started the controls, while Nikko and Mei put their helmets back on and fastened themselves into their seats.

Hiro's hands flitted across the control screen so fast that Nikko could hardly see what he was doing. He was glad he hadn't tried to fly the ship.

Within seconds, they were hurtling away.

CHAPTER 5
SAFE

Nikko heard a knock on the door of their cabin. He'd been in bed since they'd got back, but he'd only slept for a few minutes at a time. The black creatures with their bright teeth and sharp claws would appear in his dreams, and he'd wake up drenched in sweat.

But at least the creatures were only in his nightmares now. He and Mei were safely back on their own ship.

Mei was snoring quietly on the top bunk. She'd managed to sleep much more than he had.

Nikko pushed himself out of bed and went to the door.

Hiro was there. He was wearing a white T-shirt and a pair of black trousers instead of his uniform. In the light of his cabin Nikko could see thick bruises on his arms and neck. It looked painful, but he was managing to smile.

"You OK?" Nikko asked.

"I'll be fine," said Hiro. "Nothing broken."

Hiro stepped in and closed the door behind him.

"Sorry about this," he whispered. "But I was right when I guessed the Corporation would want us to give evidence about what happened. None of the other passengers know this, but we're heading back to Earth."

Nikko felt his shoulders slump. He'd known this would happen, but that didn't make it any easier.

"But the good news is that they're sending the army out to destroy that cargo ship," he said. "None of those creatures will survive."

Nikko clasped Hiro's arm. It felt hot and clammy.

"Thanks for protecting us," he said. "We'd all be dead if you hadn't reacted so quickly."

"I'm just sorry you got dragged into it," Hiro replied. "And I'm sorry it's not over yet."

Nikko shrugged.

Hiro wandered back out into the corridor.

"Who was that?" asked Mei, stirring from her sleep.

"Hiro," said Nikko. He thought about telling his sister they were going back to Earth, but he decided to let her sleep first. It was going to hit her hard.

"He feels... like he's struggling," said Mei. "That's all I can tell."

Nikko had heard that before. She'd said it about the infected people on the ship.

Nikko stuck his head out into the corridor.

Hiro was halfway down it. Nikko hadn't noticed before, but he was walking with a limp.

"Hey!" shouted Nikko.

Hiro turned around. Nikko had caught him off guard and his face was sagging. His mouth was hanging limply down and the skin around his eyes was loose. A small trickle of blood was coming out of his left eye-socket.

Hiro forced his face back into a wide grin. It was just like the smiles the infected crew members had shown them.

The last words Hiro had said echoed in Nikko's mind:

I'm sorry it's not over yet.

That's when Nikko realised they weren't safe at all. In fact, the danger was just beginning, and it was heading straight for Earth.

THE END

ABOUT THE AUTHOR

Tim Collins is originally from Manchester and now lives near Oxford. He has written more than 90 books, including Wimpy Vampire, Cosmic Colin and the Long-Lost Secret Diary of the World's Worst series. He has won awards in the UK and Germany.

ABOUT THE ARTIST

Mark Penman is a freelance illustrator, comic-book artist and art lecturer hailing from the rainy North East of England. When not writing and drawing his own comics, Mark enjoys reading horror and fantasy books and indulging in his passion for history. This interest in bygone times has led Mark to begin practising medieval longsword combat in the hope he may be whisked away to a magical kingdom where he will save it from an impending evil. Well, we all gotta daydream, right?